Flower Power

by Melody Mews

illustrated by Ellen Stubbings

LITTLE SIMON

New York London Toronto Sydney New Delhi

LITTLE SIMON
An imprint of Simon & Schuster Children's Publishing Division
1230 Avenue of the Americas, New York, New York 10020
First Little Simon paperback edition February 2022.
Designed by Laura Roode. The text of this book was set in Banda.
Manufactured in the United States of America 1221 MTN 10 9 8 7 6 5 4 3 2 1
Cataloging-in-Publication Data is available for this title from the Library of Congress.
ISBN 978-1-6659-1201-3 (hc)
ISBN 978-1-6659-1200-6 (pbk)
ISBN 978-1-6659-1202-0 (eBook)

Contents

chapter 1

The Royal Garden

It was a beautiful sunny day in Lollyland. Itty Bitty Princess Kitty and Esme Butterfly were playing in the royal garden at the palace where Itty lived.

"Ohh, look at those poppies," Esme called as she fluttered off to admire the bright orange flowers.

In Itty's opinion, the royal garden was one of the prettiest places in Lollyland. *And it's the best smelling*, Itty thought as the gentle breeze carried the perfumed scent through the air.

Itty spotted a watering can and decided that the sunflowers looked a little thirsty. She picked it up and sprinkled some cool water on them.

"Do you mind?"

Itty gasped.

"Shh! Sunny, that's the *princess* watering us!"

"Whoops, sorry, Princess Itty!" the sunflower named Sunny said.

Itty peered closely at the talking sunflowers. It was no surprise to Itty that they *could* talk—many flowers in Lollyland could. But it was a surprise that they had *chosen* to talk, because flowers usually kept to themselves.

"I'm so sorry!" Itty said. "But . . . don't you like being watered?"

shh!

"Usually, yes," Sunny said. "But it just rained. And nobody likes a soggy sunflower."

"Oh, you're just sour because no one pays attention to us

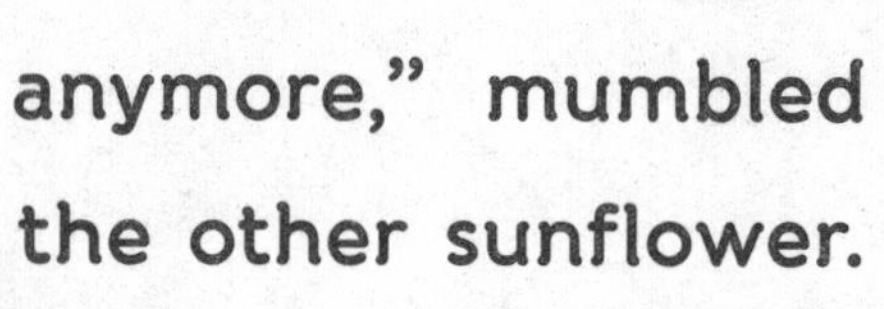

anymore," mumbled the other sunflower. Then she clapped a petal over her mouth. "I'm sorry, Princess! I shouldn't have said that!"

"It's okay," Itty assured the sunflower. "Can you tell me what you mean?"

"What Flora means is that the royal garden used to be one of the most famous places in Lollyland," Sunny blurted out. "Creatures would visit from far and wide to admire us. But lately . . ." Sunny's voice trailed off.

"Lately no one comes to visit anymore," Flora finished. "Not since the royal gardener left. Lollyland seems to have forgotten all about us."

"But I love this garden!" Itty exclaimed.

Itty noticed that the flowers around her seemed to stand just a teeny bit taller when she said that.

"Well, that's nice to hear," said Sunny. "But it sure doesn't feel like anyone else does."

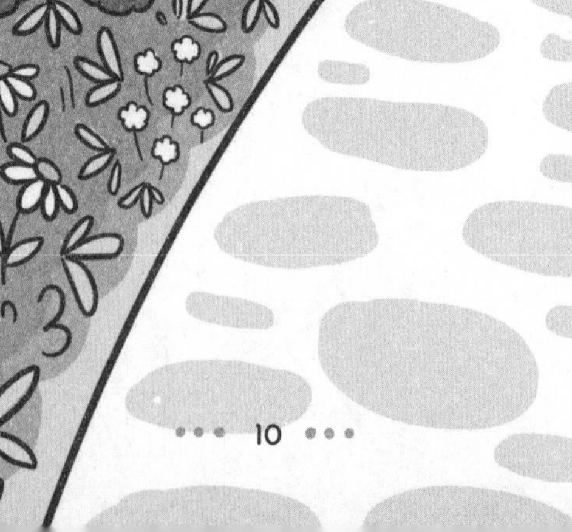

chapter 2

Flowers and Fairies

For the rest of the day, Itty couldn't stop thinking about what the sunflowers had told her.

She was so lost in thought during dinner that she barely noticed when Garbanzo, the fairy who ran the royal kitchen, placed a platter of freshly baked treats on the table for dessert.

"Itty, would you care for a cherry fudge cookie, a candy cane–glazed doughnut, or a whipped cream puff?" the Queen asked.

Itty shrugged.

Garbanzo, who was used to praise from Itty for her delicious desserts, stomped her tiny feet and flew off in a huff.

The King and Queen exchanged a concerned look.

"Is something wrong, darling?" the Queen asked as she nibbled on a fish-shaped cookie.

"Sort of," Itty began. "It's about my responsibilities. . . ."

The Queen frowned. "Itty, I'm surprised. When you became a princess, you knew that you'd have to continue to do your chores—"

"Oh, it's not that!" Itty said quickly. "It's . . . actually . . . I want *more* chores."

"I have some you can take over for me," the King said through a mouthful of cream puff.

The Queen rolled her eyes at him, then turned to Itty. "What do you have in mind, sweetie?"

"I was thinking of the garden," Itty said. She had not given this a lot of thought yet, but the words came tumbling out. "We don't have a royal gardener anymore, but someone needs to be looking after the flowers."

"That's a nice idea . . . ," the Queen said slowly. "But the flowers can be very . . . *particular.*"

"It's true. Flowers make fairies seem *easygoing*!" the King said with a chuckle.

The loud "Hmph!" from the kitchen told them that Garbanzo had heard the King's comment and did *not* find it funny.

Itty nodded. "I understand," she said. "But I'd still like to try. I know that with a little bit of work, the garden can be even *more* beautiful than it already is."

"All right, then," said the Queen. "In the meantime, your father needs to go apologize to poor Garbanzo."

Itty couldn't help but giggle as her dad walked sheepishly into the royal kitchen.

chapter 3

Princess Weed-Puller

"Thanks for offering to help me in the garden," Itty said to Esme the next day. Their cloud pulled to a gentle stop in front of the palace.

During school that day, Itty had told Esme about her plan to take care of the flowers and Esme had volunteered to help.

"So what needs to be done?" Esme asked as they headed toward the garden.

"I'm not sure," Itty admitted. "We'll have to ask the flowers."

"Hellooooo . . . ," Esme called as she circled around the flowers.

There was no response.

"Hey, it's the Princess!" a flower suddenly said. It was Sunny.

"Hi, Sunny! Hi, Flora," Itty said. "This is my friend Esme. You didn't get to meet her yesterday."

Esme waved a wing at the flowers. "I love your yellow," she told Sunny and Flora.

Itty noticed that this compliment made the flowers so happy they were practically *sparkling*.

“I have something to tell you,” Itty said excitedly to the flowers. “You’re getting a new royal gardener!”

“Who?!” cried Flora, beaming. “Who is it?”

"It's . . . me!" exclaimed Itty. "But the thing is, I'm going to need a little help. Will you two show me where to start?"

"We'd be honored," replied Sunny. "How about some . . . weeding?"

Just then, Flora and several other flowers in the garden gasped.

"You can't ask the Princess to pull weeds!" cried a petunia.

"Yeah, princesses can't get their paws dirty," added a shocked tulip.

"Oh, I don't mind getting my paws dirty!" Itty assured the flowers. "I *want* to help!"

"Me too!" Esme added.

"Well, all right," said Flora. "If you insist."

As it turned out, butterflies were not very good at pulling weeds. But Esme helped by flying around the garden to let Itty know which spots needed weeding.

On the other hand, Itty discovered that her digging skills made her an excellent weed-puller!

Before long, it wasn't just Itty's *paws* that were covered in dirt. *She* was covered in dirt from head to toe. But she didn't care. The more she worked, the more the flowers chatted about what the royal gardener used to do.

By the time Itty was finished, the garden was free of weeds *and* Itty knew exactly what else needed to be done.

chapter 4

Good Night, Garden

Itty spent all of dinner telling her parents what she had learned from the flowers.

"They like having glitter added to the soil every once in a while," Itty explained between bites of Garbanzo's special spaghetti with candied tomato sauce. "It makes their petals sparkle in the sun. And their favorite water is from Mermaid Cove, so I need to gather water from there once a week."

"Wow, I never knew any of this," the Queen remarked.

After dinner, Itty followed her parents into the royal library, where they sometimes liked to relax after meals. She was still talking about the flowers.

“They really like getting compliments,” Itty said.

“Doesn’t everyone?” The King chuckled.

"It's *really* important for the flowers," Itty explained. "And lately they've been feeling a little down. They said they don't feel like they have many admirers anymore. But I'm going to fix that!"

"I'm so proud of you, Itty," the Queen said. She patted the spot next to her on the velvet sofa. "Now why don't you curl up and read a book? You worked hard today and deserve a nice rest."

"No time to rest," Itty said. "I want to go back out to the garden to make sure the flowers have everything they need for the night. And to tell them how nice they look now that all the weeds are gone."

"Okay, sweetie," the Queen said. "Don't be out for too long. It's almost bedtime."

Itty nodded and rushed outside. The sun had set and it was beginning to get dark, but not so dark that Itty couldn't see.

It was quiet and peaceful in the garden. A gentle breeze carried the sweet perfume of the flowers through the air.

“It smells so good out here,” Itty said as she stood in the center of the garden. “And . . . it looks so nice and tidy without all the weeds . . . and you all look so beautiful in the moonlight tonight.”

Itty was pretty sure she heard the sleepy flowers sigh happily. She smiled and headed back into the palace. It was now time for *her* to get some sleep too.

chapter 5

Mermaid Cove

The next day, Itty met up with her friends at Mermaid Cove.

"Why do you have a bucket?" Luna Unicorn asked when she spotted Itty carrying a big wooden pail.

"To gather water for the royal garden," Itty explained.

"The flowers told Itty that this is their favorite water in all of Lollyland," Esme added.

"Flowers *told* you that?" Chipper Bunny repeated. He sounded surprised. Like everyone in Lollyland, Chipper knew that flowers didn't usually talk much.

"I'm becoming friends with them and they're actually pretty chatty," Itty replied. "I also found out that they like having glitter added to their soil—"

Before Itty could finish, a spurt of glitter exploded from Luna's horn and rained down on the friends, something that happened every time Luna got excited.

Which was often.

“Did you say they *like* glitter?” Luna squealed. “Did you tell them about me and my horn?”

“Not yet.” Itty giggled. “But I was planning to ask you to come visit the garden!”

Itty walked to the edge of the water and began to fill her bucket. A moment later, the surface at the center of the pond began to quiver, and then, to Itty's surprise, a mermaid popped up! She had long violet hair.

Itty heard her friends gasp behind her. Seeing a mermaid was a very special treat!

"Hello," Itty said shyly. "I hope you don't mind—I'm gathering water for the flowers in the royal garden. This is their favorite water in all of Lollyland."

"Of course I don't mind." The mermaid smiled. "That's very kind of you, Princess. Now if you'll excuse me . . ."

Then the mermaid began to sing: one, two, three, four notes. She waved and disappeared beneath the surface.

In Lollyland, mermaids sang the time. And this mermaid had just let everyone know that it was four o'clock. Itty needed to head back to the palace with her bucket of water so she could finish in the garden before dinner.

chapter 6

Itty's Idea

Over the next few weeks, Itty made several more trips to Mermaid Cove to collect water for the garden. She knew to only water the flowers on days when it hadn't rained.

Luna visited a few times and made sure the soil had all the glitter it needed.

Chipper came over and helped Itty with weeding, while Esme flew around the garden. With her butterfly's-eye view, she could alert them to any areas that needed special attention.

Itty and her friends also complimented the flowers . . . *a lot*. And it was clear how much the flowers appreciated it.

You're so tall!

I love your petals!

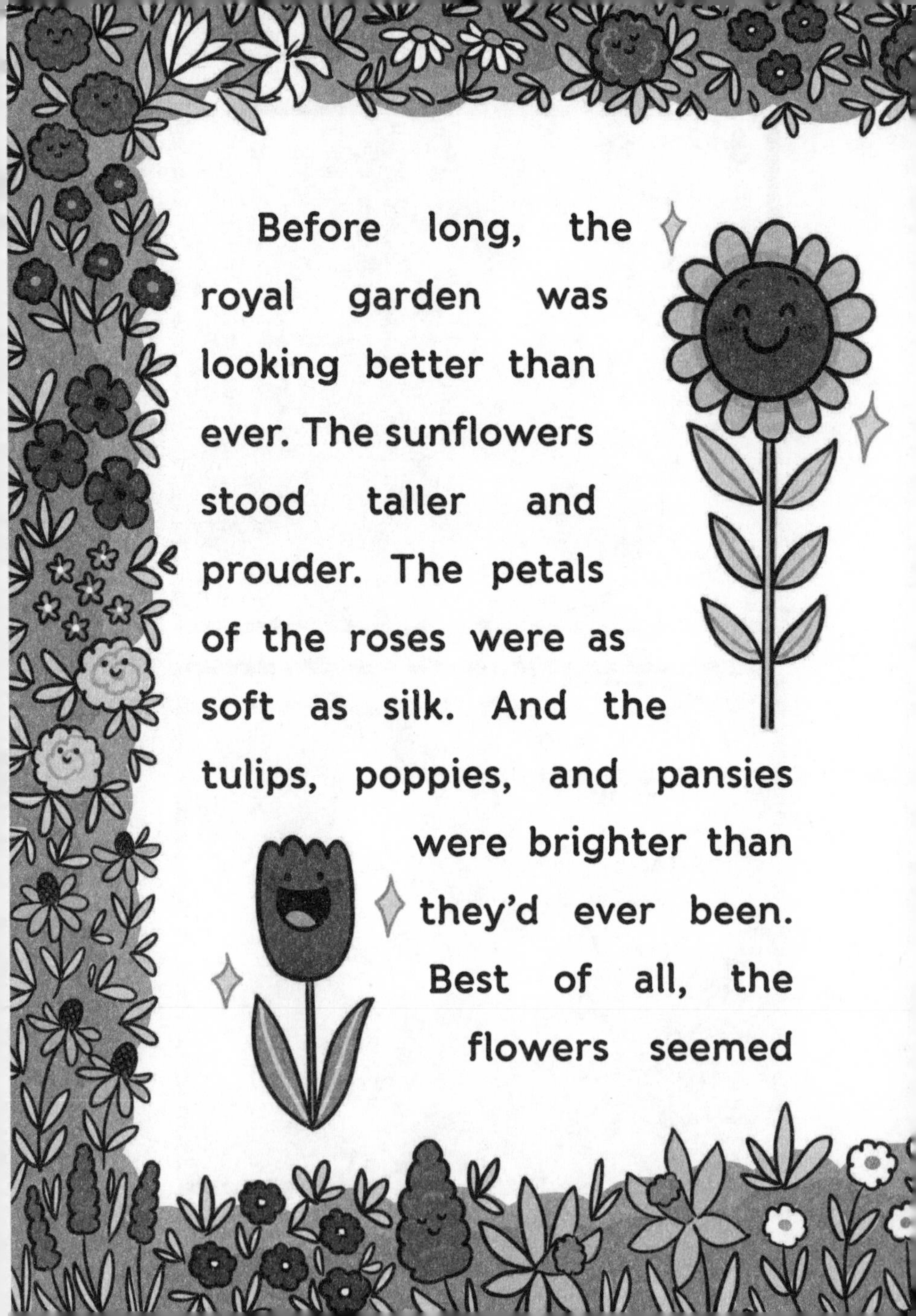

Before long, the royal garden was looking better than ever. The sunflowers stood taller and prouder. The petals of the roses were as soft as silk. And the tulips, poppies, and pansies were brighter than they'd ever been. Best of all, the flowers seemed

happier. The entire garden shimmered in the sun and the air was perfumed with the most wonderful scent Itty had ever smelled.

"You are all looking especially lovely today," Itty said to a cluster of daisies as she knelt down to smooth the soil.

"Thank you, Princess," a daisy named Peter replied proudly. "Thank you for all that you have done for this garden."

"It's my pleasure," Itty said. And she meant it. She loved helping the flowers flourish. She just wished that more of Lollyland would visit the garden and see how splendid it looked.

If only there was some way to *bring* everyone there. . . .

Just then, Itty had an idea.

"I have to go now!" Itty exclaimed as she grabbed her tools. "But I'll be back tomorrow . . . hopefully, with some very exciting news!"

chapter 7

A Garden Party?

"A garden party?" Queen Kitty tapped her paws on her desk, which Itty knew meant she was considering it. "Hmmm . . ."

"It *has* been a while since we had a party at the palace," the King said.

"Not since the royal ball when I became princess," Itty added. She had just told her parents about her idea: to throw a garden party and invite all of Lollyland!

“We’ll need to let Garbanzo know immediately so we can begin planning the menu,” the Queen continued.

Itty grinned. If her mom was thinking about the menu, that meant the party was going to happen.

"And we need to get out invitations," added the King. "But I can handle that. Oh, Jubilee! Come here please!" he boomed.

Moments later Jubilee, the royal announcement fairy, flew into the study.

"Hello there!" Itty's dad greeted the little fairy. "We've just decided we're going to have a garden party in . . ." The King paused.

"In one week," Itty finished.

The Queen nodded.

"And we'd like to invite all of Lollyland," the King added.

"That doesn't give my fairies very much time," Jubilee grumbled. But despite his grumbling, Itty could tell that he was excited.

Fairies loved a good party as much as anyone else.

"Thank you, Jubilee!" her father called as the fairy flew away.

"Can I tell my friends?" Itty asked.

"Yes, of course," her mother responded. "Now that your father has ordered the invitations and you'll be getting the garden ready,

I suppose I'm the one who must break the news to Garbanzo that she's going to be cooking for all of Lollyland."

"Good luck!" Itty and her dad called in unison.

Then Itty dashed after Jubilee. She needed him to send messenger fairies to her friends' houses so they'd know to meet her at Goodie Grove. It was time for some serious party planning!

chapter 8

Party Planning Time!

"Remember not to let your announcement fairies know that *you* already know about the party!" Itty warned. It was a little while later, and Itty and her friends were gathered in Goodie Grove.

Announcement fairies did *not*

like when their announcements were spoiled.

"This is so exciting!" Luna exclaimed, glitter raining down. "So, how can we help?"

"Let's get snacks first," Chipper suggested. "I think better when I'm not hungry."

The friends scattered to choose their snacks, which were plentiful in Goodie Grove.

Itty chose a raspberry lollipop from a nearby bush and rejoined her friends.

"So what do you need us to do?" Esme asked as everyone got comfortable in the grass with their snacks.

"Well, my mom is working with Garbanzo on the food," Itty began. "And the announcement fairies will invite everyone. But I was thinking it could be fun to have a performance. It could even be a surprise for the flowers."

"What about a butterfly dance?" Esme suggested.

“That’s a wonderful idea!” Itty cheered.

“I love it!” Chipper shouted.

The glitter that came from Luna’s horn made it clear that she agreed too.

Itty gasped. "I just realized something," she said. "There won't be *any* party if I don't go tell the flowers about it right away!" Itty jumped up to hail a cloud. She said a quick goodbye to her friends and dashed back to the palace.

When they heard the news, the flowers were even more excited than Itty had expected.

But then the worrying began.

“What will we do about food?” fretted a pansy.

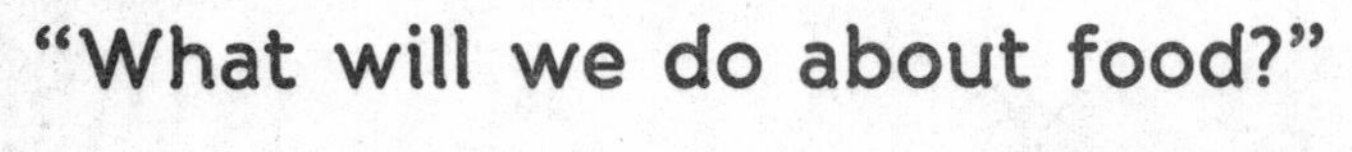

"And don't we need music?" asked a lilac.

"It's all being taken care of," Itty assured the flowers. "You will all be the stars of the show. Or . . . the flowers of the fete!"

chapter 9

Ready, Set, Grow!

The next few days flew by in a blur of party planning. From making sure the garden was looking its finest and the flowers were happy, to creating the decorations, to picking Itty's outfit—which Luna was more than happy to help out with—there was much to do!

The morning of the party, Itty put on the pink and yellow floral sundress Luna had chosen and hurried downstairs. The guests would be arriving soon.

Itty paused at the bottom of the stairs. Delicious smells were coming out of the royal kitchen. Itty decided she ought to take a peek to see how things were going. Perhaps Garbanzo needed some help, or even a taste-tester?

What Itty saw inside the kitchen took her breath away! Garbanzo and the other food fairies had baked *hundreds* of cupcakes. They were all piped with beautiful

frosting flowers that looked like the real flowers in the garden.

There were trays piled high with meringue pies, colorful berry tarts, and spongy marshmallow cookies.

Itty's mouth watered. She looked around the kitchen. Garbanzo was busy supervising some fairies who were brewing tea.

Itty reached for a cookie . . .

"Don't do it!"

Itty was surprised to see her dad crouching behind her in the kitchen.

"Garbanzo caught me twice already," he whispered. "Chased me with a rolling pin!"

"Then what are you doing in here?" Itty asked.

"Third time's the charm?" The King shrugged.

Itty giggled and decided she could wait a little longer to taste everything. She left the kitchen and joined her mother on the balcony at the front of the palace.

The garden below sparkled in the sunlight. It had never looked more radiant than it did today. Tables and chairs were set up all around so guests could sit and enjoy the splendor of the flowers.

Itty saw the royal photographer and royal portrait painter roaming about, waiting for the guests to arrive.

The Queen turned to Itty and smiled. "It's time," she said. "Are you ready?"

chapter 10

The Flowers' Surprise

"I've never seen such beautiful flowers," said an elegant peacock in a sun hat.

"The colors are absolutely stunning," agreed a hedgehog in a striped suit.

"The only thing more divine is that scent in the air," said a hummingbird.

The party was a huge success and Itty was delighted. All of Lollyland had showed up, and everyone agreed that the garden looked splendid. The flowers stood tall and proud, basking in the compliments they were receiving.

As the royal musicians finished the song they were playing, the piano player clapped his hands. Itty knew the signal: The performance was about to begin!

The band began to play a new song, and a group of butterflies flew to the center of the garden. They swooped up and down, in and out, creating patterns and flower shapes in the air as the guests cheered.

“The butterflies are doing this for us!” exclaimed Flora.

“Wow. They’re amazing,” added Sunny, swaying to the music.

"Well, we wanted you to know how much Lollyland appreciates you," Itty said to her flower friends. "And I have some more news."

Earlier in the party, Itty's parents had asked her what she thought about throwing a garden party every spring. And not just that—but opening the garden to the creatures of Lollyland every *weekend*. Itty had told her parents she'd ask the flowers, but she already knew what their answer would be.

"YES!" Sunny and Flora cried together. And Itty saw their yellow petals glow brighter than ever.

If you like Itty's adventures, then you'll love . . .